The Olympics!

This was Lisa's big chance! If she did well at the big gymnastic meet, Lisa would be one step closer to making the Olympic team. And Jeff was finally paying attention to her. It was the dream of her lifetime.

But when Lisa goes for her pre-competition physical, the doctor finds something wrong with her back. Lisa may even have to wear a brace. And she may have to give up gymnastics.

Maybe when I wake up, Lisa prays, this will all be a bad dream . . .

Nothing Hurts But My Heart is required reading for every boy and girl (and their distraught parents) who learn that bracing may be needed to treat their scoliosis. It is a moving true-to-life story about the impact such news had on young Lisa's life. In her book, Linda Barr gives wonderfully honest insight into the real issues important to the adolescent facing this extraordinary challenge.

Nothing Hurts But My Heart is enjoyable reading for all young people. The book offers hope to get through difficult situations and shows the meaning and importance of encouragement, support, and good friends.

Joseph O'Brien, President
National Scoliosis Foundation

Nothing Hurts But My Heart

LINDA BARR

To my late parents, Paul and Audrey Gimbel, who gave me more support than a straight spine ever could

And to my daughter, Colleen, who is like me in many ways

Special Thanks to:

The National Scoliosis Foundation, for providing information on current treatment methods

David Kozersky, C.P.O., who showed me how braces are fitted these days

Scott Ryan, Assistant Coach at Buckeye Gymnastics in Westerville, Ohio, who helped with the gymnastics aspect of the story

Published by Willowisp Press
801 94th Avenue North, St. Petersburg, Florida 33702

Printed in the United States of America

2 4 6 8 10 9 7 5 3 1

ISBN 0-87406-722-7

One

LISA Conklin steadied herself at one end of the narrow balance beam and took a deep breath. She had practiced back walkovers a hundred times. They still weren't easy, but they were compulsory at the big gymnastics meet coming up. She had to bend all the way backward and grab the balance beam behind her. Then she had to swing her legs over her body and stand up again. She had learned the move on a practice beam that was flat against the gym floor. But now she could do it on the real beam—four and a half feet up in the air. The coach had told her that after she could do back walkovers perfectly, she'd be ready to try a back handspring to a back layout. That was much harder!

Lisa glanced down at the three little girls in black leotards who were watching every move she made. I used to feel nervous when the kids from the younger gymnastics class watched me, Lisa remembered, but now I don't mind at all. Sometimes even the girls from her own class watched her. Lisa always seemed to be the first one in the class to try a new movement or a new combination. She smiled at the little girls. They looked at each other and giggled.

Out of the corner of her eye, Lisa could see Jeff, the best-looking boy in her math class. He was leaning against the back wall of the gym with his arms crossed. Even though Jeff's dark hair was still wet from swim practice, Lisa thought he was good-looking anyway.

Suddenly Lisa's heart skipped a beat. Jeff was looking at her! Now I'm nervous! she thought. She pulled her leotard down in the back and brushed her short brown bangs back from her face. Maybe I can string two walkovers together, like I did on Wednesday, she thought. Maybe that would impress him!

Lisa gracefully stretched both arms high over her head. Then she lifted her right leg as high as possible and leaned over backward, bringing her arms down behind her until she could grab the narrow balance beam.

"Keep those legs straight, Lisa!" Mrs. Pogue, her coach, called.

Lisa smiled as she concentrated on keeping her balance. Mrs. Pogue had coached Lisa in gymnastics every Monday, Wednesday, and Friday for over three years. She reminds me to keep my legs straight at least twice a lesson, Lisa thought, but at least she's paying attention. That really helps. Lisa shifted her weight to her hands and lifted her left foot off the beam. She balanced on both hands for half a second with her legs in a split position. Then she brought her right foot down on the narrow beam and stood up again. Lisa smoothly swung her left leg up for the second walkover. She would have made it, too, except as she balanced on her hands the second time, she turned her head slightly to see if Jeff were still watching.

She was off balance! Before Lisa knew it, she was falling. She hit the mat under the beam with a loud thud. Lisa quickly glanced toward the back wall of the gym. Just her luck! Jeff was still watching her, and grinning, too!

"Are you hurt, Lisa?" Lisa was surprised to see her father reaching down to help her up. He looked worried.

"No, I'm okay!" She quickly got to her feet. "You're early today, Dad!" This just isn't my day! Lisa told herself. Dad saw me fall, too.

Lisa's dad sold insurance, and he had arranged his schedule so he could pick her up after gymnastics every Friday. She always thought his business suit looked out of place in the sweaty, noisy gym, but he never missed a Friday. "I came a few minutes early so I could watch my best girl!" he told her today.

Lisa smiled a little at his old joke. She wasn't just his "best" girl, she was the Conklins' only child. Then she sighed. "I did those walkovers perfectly on Wednesday, Dad," she said.

"Don't worry about it, honey. Everyone falls sometimes," he said as he brushed chalk off her shoulder. "Even experts like you!"

Mrs. Pogue came over and patted Lisa's arm. A few strands of the coach's gray hair had escaped from the bun perched on top of her head. Lisa had decided long ago that Mrs. Pogue must have twenty pairs of the white shorts and long-sleeved white tops that she wore to the gym every day.

"Lisa is doing exceptionally well," the coach told Lisa's father. "None of the other girls has even tried a stunt like that. I think she's just about ready for those regional gymnastic trials next month."

"She'll do great," Lisa's father agreed. "After all, she won first place in the state meet this year. Just wait until those judges at the regionals see her!" He gave Lisa a quick hug. She knew her dad loved to watch her compete.

She guessed it reminded him of the years when he was a track star in college. A whole shelf in their family room was filled with his trophies.

"Lisa will have some stiff competition," Mrs. Pogue remarked, "but if her scores are high enough at the regionals, the next step is the nationals. If she does well at the nationals, she'll even have a chance to be on the U.S. Olympic team!"

"The Olympics!" Lisa whispered. She glanced up at her dad, who was smiling and nodding. "I really need to work on my balance beam routine," she said.

"What if I put a practice beam in your bedroom?" her father offered. "Your ceiling is nice and high, so there's plenty of room. That way you could work out at home."

Lisa nodded. Those extra hours of practice will help me win at the regionals. I'll do anything for a chance at the Olympics!

I've got to make sure Jeff finds out about my chance at the Olympics, Lisa told herself. He'll be really impressed! How can I let him know? Maybe Megan can help think of a way when she stays over tonight!

"Don't forget to have your doctor fill out that medical form for the regionals," Mrs. Pogue reminded Lisa's dad. "If Lisa hasn't had a physical exam lately, your doctor will have to give her one before she can compete."

"We'll take care of that right away," Mr. Conklin said. He smiled at his daughter.

Two

"LISA, could you possibly take a break now?" Megan asked. "You've been doing walk-back-overs or whatever you call them for at least twenty hours!" Megan was dressed in an extra-large T-shirt. She was sitting cross-legged on Lisa's bed, carefully painting her fingernails bright red.

Lisa was dressed in a purple leotard. She was balancing on her hands on the new practice beam her father had set up as soon as they got home from gymnastics.

The four-inch-wide board stretched across the rug from her bed to the doorway. It made walking through the room harder and Lisa had accidentally kicked one of her teddy bears off her dresser, but it was worth it. Lisa was sure that this extra practice would make a big difference in her score at the regionals.

Lisa's mom knocked lightly on the bedroom

door and opened it halfway. She was wearing her old quilted robe, the same one Lisa could remember snuggling against when she was little. "Your dad and I are going to bed, Lisa. Why don't you two think about getting some sleep, too. Okay?"

"Can't we stay up just a little longer, Mom?" Lisa begged.

Her mom smiled and nodded. "Okay, just a little longer. See you in the morning!" She closed the door again.

"Just a few more walkovers," Lisa said. "Then let's go downstairs and get something to eat."

"That's a great idea!" Megan said. "I had dinner at home, but I'm still starving!"

"No wonder! You should have eaten lunch today," Lisa told her. Today at lunch, Lisa noticed that Megan hadn't eaten a thing.

Megan made a face. "I couldn't! I have health class just before lunch and we talked about skin diseases. Who can eat after that?" Megan shook her head and blew on her fingernails.

"Oh, that reminds, me, Lisa," Megan said suddenly. "Look at this pimple on my chin. Does it look like a skin disease to you?" Being careful not to smear her fingernail polish, Megan pointed to the blemish.

Lisa leaned on the bed and took a look.

"Looks like a plain, ordinary pimple to me, Meg. Actually, it blends right in with your freckles. I think it's your imagination again."

"Well, if you say so," Megan said slowly. "You have to be careful, though. There's a lot of stuff going around. My new makeup will cover it anyway." Megan started painting her toenails red as Lisa leaned backward into another walkover.

"You should see what my mom bought herself when she got me that makeup," Megan said. "Jeans just like your new ones. At her age!"

"Gross!" Lisa managed to say as she balanced on her hands. "Mothers should stick to corduroy pants and heavy sweaters."

Megan nodded. "Do you think our mothers wore jeans when they were teenagers?" she wondered. "It's hard to imagine my mother any age but old!"

"I know!" Lisa agreed. She smiled as she finished the second walkover without a hitch. "There's a shoebox of old pictures in the den downstairs. Let's bring it up. I think there are some pictures in it of my parents when they were teenagers."

Soon the girls were creeping through the darkened house to the kitchen for a bag of pretzels. They sneaked into the den and grabbed the shoebox full of pictures. Then the two friends tiptoed back to Lisa's bedroom.

They sat on the bed and giggled at an old picture of Lisa's mom and her friends taken when they were in high school. The girls were all wearing short, ruffled pajamas and lying around on sleeping bags on the floor. Most of them had their hair in rollers. "That's at my grandma's house," Lisa told Megan. "Can you believe it? My mom had slumber parties, too!"

Megan giggled again and picked up another picture. "Who's that?"

The picture showed a girl about their age lying on a bed in a thick cast. You could see only the top half of her body. The cast went up to her chin and around the back of her head. Only her face and arms were free. She had turned on her side to face the camera. There was a sad smile on her face.

"It's my mother," Lisa said quietly. "She had some kind of operation on her back. I guess she had to be in that cast for a long time."

Megan held the picture up to the light. "You know what, Lisa? Your mom looks almost like you in that picture!"

"Oh, great, Meg! Just what I wanted to hear!" Lisa said. She took the picture from Megan and tossed it in the shoebox. "Aren't you tired? Let's go to sleep." Lisa turned off the light.

"Okay," Megan said, "but you didn't tell me yet if you saw Jeff at the gym today." She got under the covers. "Did you? Was Steve with him?"

"Jeff was watching when I fell off the beam," Lisa said with a sigh. "I didn't see Steve. Jeff probably thinks I'm the biggest klutz in the whole school." Lisa propped herself up on one elbow. "Help me, Meg. We've got to think of some way to let Jeff know I'm a good enough gymnast to be going to the regionals."

Megan thought for a minute. "I know!" She sat up in bed. "I'll call Jeff's house. He doesn't know my voice. When he answers, I'll say, 'Did you hear Lisa Conklin's been picked for the regional gymnastic trials, John?' He'll say, 'I'm not John,' and I'll say, 'Sorry, wrong number!'" Megan began to giggle.

Lisa was smiling in the darkness. "I don't think Jeff will be fooled, Meg."

"Oh, come on. I know it will work!" Megan insisted. "Why don't we try it Tuesday after school? You don't have gymnastics then. You could listen while I call him, but you have to promise not to make me laugh!"

Lisa shook her head. "I can't do it Tuesday.

My mom made a doctor's appointment for me then. I have to have a physical before the regionals."

"A physical?" Megan's voice suddenly sounded very serious. "What if the doctor finds something wrong with you?"

"Oh, Megan!" Lisa pulled the covers up and closed her eyes. *Megan sure has a wild imagination*, she thought as she fell asleep.

Three

"MOM, could I go in by myself this time?" Lisa asked. "I'm thirteen now, you know." Lisa and her mother were sitting in their family doctor's waiting room. Lisa knew Dr. O'Neil would ask her to get undressed for the physical exam and she wanted as few people as possible around when that happened. She hated for anyone, even her mother, to see her naked. It didn't even help that Dr. O'Neil was a woman. Those paper robes the nurse always told you to put on weren't much good, either.

Her mom put down her magazine and sighed. "I really would rather come in with you, Lisa, but I guess Dr. O'Neil will tell me anything I need to know."

Lisa nodded and smiled nervously. She wished the whole thing were over.

Her mother handed her the medical form

for the regional trials. "Why don't you ask the doctor to fill this out?" Mrs. Conklin suggested.

Lisa was glad to think about something besides the physical. "I can't wait for the regionals, Mom! I've really been working so hard that I just know I'll get a high score! I'll bet my picture will be in our paper again, just like after the state meet. Maybe this time reporters will come to interview me!" Lisa smiled at her mother. "They might even ask you what it's like to be the mother of a top gymnast!"

Lisa's mom reached over and squeezed her shoulder. "That would really be exciting, Lisa," she agreed, smiling, "but let's wait to see what happens at the regionals before we plan too far ahead."

Lisa frowned. Sometimes her mother was no fun at all.

"Lisa Conklin?" a nurse called out. Oh no, Lisa thought. It's my turn! She took a big breath and smiled bravely at her mom. Then she followed the nurse down a hallway to an examining room. As soon as the nurse left her alone in the room, Lisa pulled her clothes off and put on the stiff paper robe. At least the nurse had let her keep her underpants on!

Lisa sat on the edge of a padded table. The

robe was long enough to reach all the way down to her knees, but somehow it still wouldn't stay closed in the back. The room was freezing. Lisa hugged herself and watched her bare legs shiver as she waited for Dr. O'Neil.

Finally the door opened, and Dr. O'Neil came in. She wore her hair in soft blond curls, but she still looked like a doctor in that long white coat with her stethoscope around her neck. Lisa remembered the first time she had seen Dr. O'Neil. She had mistaken her for the nurse. Lisa hoped she didn't remember that.

Lisa pulled her paper robe tighter around her. Please let this be over quickly, she prayed. Why don't doctors put you to sleep for physicals the way they do for operations?

"Well, Lisa, how are the gymnastics going?" Dr. O'Neil asked.

"Great!" Lisa said as she handed the doctor the medical form.

"Regional trials, huh?" Dr. O'Neil read. She looked at Lisa. "You must be very good!" Lisa grinned and stopped holding her robe so tightly. Maybe, just maybe, she thought, I'll live through this physical after all.

Dr. O'Neil talked nonstop while she examined Lisa. She warned her about the icy stethoscope and asked about school and her "boyfriends." Finally, she got to the subject Lisa had been dreading. No, Lisa told her, her periods were not regular yet. In fact, she told herself, they were always a surprise. Usually they surprised her in the middle of English class.

"Do you still have cramps or pain with your periods?" Dr. O'Neil asked. Lisa was lying on her back on the padded table while the doctor poked her stomach.

Lisa thought about the pain she felt when she dropped her purse in history class and Mike Freeland saw her emergency supplies fall out. She guessed that wasn't the pain Dr. O'Neil meant. "Not very often," she answered.

The doctor helped Lisa to her feet. "Now let's check your back. Gymnasts need strong backs, right? Turn around and bend forward," she instructed. "That's it. Let your hands hang down in front of you and keep them together."

Dr. O'Neil ran her fingers down Lisa's back bone. Lisa waited for her to say something as she had during the rest of the exam. But Dr. O'Neil said nothing. Instead the doctor turned her back to Lisa and wrote something on Lisa's chart.

"Stand up straight now, Lisa. Let your arms just hang at your sides." Dr. O'Neil put her hands on Lisa's shoulders, then on her hips.

She ran her fingers down both sides of Lisa's spine again. The room was very quiet. She wrote something else on the chart.

"Okay, you can get dressed," Dr. O'Neil said as she patted Lisa's shoulder. "I want to talk to you and your mom in my office."

Lisa started to ask if anything were wrong, but she decided not to. What could be wrong, anyway? Nothing hurts—nothing at all.

As soon as the doctor left, Lisa threw off the paper robe and got dressed as fast as she could. When she went out into the hallway, the nurse was standing there.

"Your mother is waiting in Dr. O'Neil's office, Lisa." She pointed at an open door. "Go on in. The doctor will be right there."

Her mom was sitting in a chair across from the doctor's desk. She was frowning. "Did the doctor find anything wrong? The nurse asked me to wait in here."

"I . . . I don't think so, Mom," Lisa said. She sat in the chair closest to her mother.

Dr. O'Neil came in, smiled at them both, and leaned against her desk. "Lisa is certainly growing into a lovely young lady, Mrs. Conklin."

Lisa's mother nodded and asked, "Is there a problem, Doctor?" Lisa thought her mother's voice sounded funny, kind of nervous.

"Well, I'm not sure, but I want Lisa to see

a specialist. Mrs. Conklin, you have scoliosis, don't you?" Dr. O'Neil asked gently.

Lisa quickly looked at her mother, who closed her eyes without answering. It seemed like forever before Mrs. Conklin opened her eyes and slowly nodded.

Lisa turned back to Dr. O'Neil. "Mom isn't sick," she said, "and I'm not either!"

"Neither one of you is sick, Lisa. Scoliosis means curvature of the spine," Dr. O'Neil explained. "Your backbone seems to be curving a little sideways instead of growing straight. Your mother has the same problem."

"I hoped this wouldn't happen," Mrs. Conklin said softly. "Lisa is so athletic. . . ."

"That's right," Lisa told Dr. O'Neil. "Mom is out of shape and her back gets stiff sometimes, but I'm a gymnast! I exercise for hours every day! I won't get like that! She just needs more exercise!"

Lisa's mother put her arm around her. "Exercise by itself won't cure scoliosis, honey," she said, almost in a whisper. Lisa thought she could see tears in her mother's eyes.

Then Lisa remembered the picture of her mother in the heavy cast. *She looks just like you,* Megan had said. Suddenly Lisa's head felt light, as if it were going to float off her shoulders. The doctor's office started turning black, and Lisa slipped toward the floor.

Lisa felt Dr. O'Neil catch her and push her back in the chair. The doctor held Lisa's head down between the girl's knees. The blackness started to fade away. Lisa realized her mother was rubbing her back and talking to her. "I didn't mean to scare you, Lisa. Everything's going to be all right. I promise!" her mother was saying.

After a minute, Lisa stopped feeling so dizzy and she sat up. She felt sweaty. Her clothes were sticking to her body. She could see worry in her mother's eyes.

Dr. O'Neil tipped Lisa's face up and looked at her carefully. "You just fainted for a second. You'll be okay now," she said. The doctor stepped back and leaned against her desk again.

"Scoliosis does sound scary," Dr. O'Neil explained, "but most people who have it don't need any treatment at all. They just need to be checked every few months while they're between the ages of ten and fifteen and growing fast to be sure their spines don't start to curve more.

Lisa swallowed and nodded. Everything is going to be okay, she told herself.

"In fact, several kids in your class probably have scoliosis," Dr. O'Neil added. "One out of every ten people has it, but most of them never know and never even need to know."

"My back doesn't hurt!" Lisa told her. "Honest! I probably wouldn't need to know either. If we hadn't come here today, I never would have known!" She looked at her mom and the doctor. The doctor smiled.

"I believe your back doesn't hurt," she said, "but I still want you to go to an orthopedist. He can tell whether you need any treatment at this point. Some teenagers, only two or three out of a thousand, have curves that can possibly get worse quickly."

"What happens to them?" Lisa asked softly.

"Those kids need to wear a brace during their growing years to stop their backs from curving more," Dr. O'Neil explained. "About one person out of a thousand with scoliosis develops a curve that even a brace won't help. Only surgery will stop it from getting worse."

"When I was your age, honey," Lisa's mom said, "I had to have the surgery. My curvature was getting worse fast. I had to have an operation to fuse the curved part of my spine into one solid piece of bone. Now that part of my back doesn't bend, but it won't curve any more either."

"Is that when you wore that big cast?" Lisa asked in a small voice.

Mrs. Conklin smiled a little. "You mean that old picture of me in bed?"

Lisa nodded. She wished she had never seen that picture.

"That cast held my back straight after the operation," her mom said, "like a cast on a broken leg."

Lisa's mom paused. "If I hadn't had that surgery, my back would have kept curving," she said slowly. "By now, I'm sure I would have been all bent over, maybe even in a wheelchair."

Lisa stared at her mother. She couldn't imagine her in a wheelchair. She shook her head to get the thought out of her mind.

"Things are different now, though," Dr. O'Neil added. "We have easier ways to help backs grow straight. Why don't you see an orthopedist right away, so you know what the situation is?"

Mrs. Conklin sighed and nodded. "Could you recommend a good one?" she asked the doctor. Her voice was so low Lisa could barely hear her mother.

She saw her mom's hand shake a little as she wrote down the orthopedist's name and phone number. I just know my back is okay, Lisa told herself. I bet I was just standing crooked.

On the way home in the car, Lisa suddenly remembered why they had gone to the doctor in the first place. "Mom, we forgot the medical form."

Her mother didn't answer. She seemed to be lost in her own thoughts. Lisa hoped her mom wouldn't run into anything with the car. She sure didn't seem to be concentrating on her driving "Mom, what about the form for the regionals? Lisa asked again.

"Oh, the form," her mother repeated. "Well," she finally said, "let's not worry about it until we talk to the orthopedist, honey."

Great, Lisa thought. We're going to have to make another trip back here to get that form. Why is Mom making such a big thing out of this? I hope we can wait until after the regionals for this appointment. I need all the time I can get to practice my routines.

Maybe Mom and Dad would let me go to the gym on Tuesdays and Thursdays, too, just until the regionals are over. Then, Lisa promised herself with a smile, I'll take a break before I start practicing for the nationals!

Four

LISA followed her mom into the house. "How are my girls today?" her father called from the living room. When he saw the look on his wife's face, he immediately put down his newspaper.

"Dr. O'Neil thinks Lisa might have scoliosis," Mrs. Conklin told him quietly. "She wants her to see an orthopedist to make sure."

Mr. Conklin stared at his wife. Then he turned to Lisa.

"I think I was just standing crooked, Dad," she said.

At first her father didn't say anything, but then he said, "I'm sure the orthopedist will say you're fine, Lisa. Your back sure hasn't stopped you in gymnastics. Dr. O'Neil is probably just being cautious."

Lisa glanced at her mom. Mrs. Conklin was frowning at her dad. Lisa looked away. Dad's right, she thought. Mom will come around after the orthopedist checks me.

At dinner a little later Lisa cut her pork chop into tiny pieces and pushed them around her plate. She noticed that her parents weren't very hungry either. Her dad was lining up his peas in a row with his fork. No one spoke.

Finally she had to ask. "What causes scoliosis? Can you catch it from someone? Could I catch it from you, Mom?"

Her mom smiled a little. "Not really, honey. It's not contagious, but it does tend to run in families."

Lisa thought for a minute. "You mean, if you didn't have scoliosis, I wouldn't get it either?" she asked.

Her mother looked surprised by her question. "Not necessarily, Lisa," she finally said. "No one in my family had it that I know of, but I got it anyway. In most cases, no one knows what causes it. The spine just starts to curve."

Lisa stared at her glass of milk. She didn't feel like drinking it, but she decided she'd better. She wondered how many glasses she'd have to drink to keep her bones from growing crooked. I probably have Dad's bones, she thought. This trip to the orthopedist is all for nothing.

"Could we go to the orthopedist after the regionals are over?" she asked.

"No," her mother answered immediately. "I want you to go as soon as possible. This is important."

Lisa tried to ignore the serious tone in her mother's voice. "But the appointment will take time away from my gymnastics! I really need to practice after school every day," she told her parents.

"Now, Lisa," her father said, "once we get this settled, your mom will stop worrying. Maybe you were standing crooked in Dr. O'Neil's office, or maybe you have a slight curve that won't change anything. There's still a good chance you can go to the regionals."

Lisa couldn't believe her ears! "A good chance?" she repeated. "Of course I'm going! I've worked too hard! I can't miss the regionals now. Everyone's counting on me!" Lisa's voice started to shake. "Don't you want me to go, Dad?"

Her father reached over and squeezed her hand. "Of course! I can't imagine that anything is seriously wrong with your back, anyway."

"George," her mother said as she put her fork down. She spoke very quietly. "I really think we need to hear what the orthopedist has to say." Lisa knew her mother was warning her father not to say anymore.

Lisa stood up. "I'm full," she said in a tight little voice. "Excuse me, please."

"Lisa, you hardly. . . ," her father called, but Lisa was already halfway up the stairs to her room.

Lisa closed her bedroom door and blinked away her tears. She hated to hear her parents argue, especially when they argued over her. If I had just stood up straight at Dr. O'Neil's office, she told herself, none of this would have happened!

She quickly changed into a leotard and started going through her warm-up exercises. I wish I had more room in here so I could practice my floor exercises, too, she thought. Maybe I could practice three back walkovers in a row on the beam, though. That will impress the judges at the regionals!

The first time she tried it, her foot hit her bed on the last walkover. She ended up sprawled on the carpet.

"Owww!" she muttered to herself as she grabbed her knee. Sharp pains were shooting through her leg.

The phone rang downstairs. "Lisa!" her mother called. "It's Megan!"

Lisa stood up on her good leg and hopped

down the hall to the phone in her parents' bedroom. I won't tell Megan what Dr. O'Neil said yet, she decided. After the orthopedist says I'm fine, I'll tell her and we'll both have a big laugh!

Megan started talking even before Lisa had a chance to say hello. "Lisa, I've thought of another way to let Jeff know you're going to be in the regionals!"

"How?" she asked Megan.

"We could ask them to put it in the school newspaper!" Megan suggested. "They like that kind of news!"

"Maybe." Lisa tried her best to sound normal.

"What's wrong?" Megan asked. "Are you sick? Oh yeah, I remember! You had your physical today!" Megan suddenly was very serious. "What did the doctor say?"

"I'm fine, Meg."

"You are?" Lisa thought Meg sounded disappointed. "You know, I was thinking maybe I should have a physical," Megan said. "My chest still looks like a boy's. Maybe there's something wrong with my hormones."

Lisa wished that was all she had to worry about. "Meg, I'm tired. I think I'll go to bed now." She yawned. She really did feel sleepy.

"Okay! See you at lunch tomorrow," Megan

said. "We still have to decide which movie we want to see this weekend."

Lisa hopped back to her room and got ready for bed. I want to see a really romantic movie this week, she told herself, with lots of kissing. That would help me forget about my real life for a while!

"I'm going to bed now," Lisa yelled down the stairs.

"Sleep tight, Lisa, and keep your chin up!" her father called.

A few minutes later her mom came up and tucked the covers in around her daughter.

"Goodnight, sweetie," her mother said. She kissed Lisa on the forehead. "I know you're worried about your gymnastics, but everything will work out for the best. I promise!"

Lisa lay in the darkness after her mom left. How can she understand about gymnastics? Lisa asked herself. I have never seen her play a sport. I'm not going to spend the rest of my life sitting around!

Lisa felt a hot tear slide out of each eye and run into her ears. At least Dad realizes how important gymnastics are to me, she thought. He won't let some dumb little problem keep me out of the regionals. He's on my side.

Five

THE earliest Lisa's mom could get an appointment with the orthopedist was the following Monday afternoon. Lisa counted the days she had to wait—five. Five too many, she thought.

The rest of the week she daydreamed through her classes. She spent the evenings in her room, practicing gymnastics and doing whatever homework she couldn't avoid. First she wished Monday would come sooner. Then she wished it wouldn't come at all. At least after this stupid appointment, she told herself, I can concentrate on the regionals and forget about doctors!

At lunch on Thursday, Lisa was staring at her tuna fish sandwich, wondering whether she would have to get undressed for the orthopedist, when Megan suddenly said, "You're not listening! I told you all about my new exercises, but you haven't heard a word!"

Lisa tried to remember what Megan had been talking about. She couldn't. "You're doing exercises, Megan?"

Megan looked annoyed. "I told you! They're for my chest! You know!"

When Lisa just looked at her blankly, Megan whispered, "I'm trying to work up to a bigger bra size! I'd show you some of the exercises, but *they* might know what they're for." She nodded at a table in the corner that was full of boys. Lisa could see Jeff sitting beside Steve. They were all laughing and shooting straw papers at each other.

Megan leaned closer to Lisa. "If these exercises don't work, I'm going to go to the doctor and find out what's really wrong!"

Suddenly Lisa felt all her anger bubble up. "Megan, you are perfectly healthy!"

Megan looked hurt. "I guess I can't expect you to understand. You have a chest!" she whispered hoarsely. Then she shook her head and said, "Lisa, you've been acting weird for at least two days now. What's going on?"

"Nothing, Megan. I . . . I'm sorry!" Lisa tried to smile. "Don't be mad at me. I hope your exercises work." The bell rang. Lunch time was over. Lisa was glad to go to math class and escape Megan's puzzled look.

* * * * *

At gymnastics on Friday, Mrs. Pogue was watching when Lisa smoothly strung two walkovers together on the balance beam.

"You've really been working hard, Lisa! Very nice!" Mrs. Pogue said.

"That's nothing!" Lisa called. "I can do three! Watch this!" She moved toward the far end of the balance beam.

"Wait, Lisa! That's too dangerous!" Mrs. Pogue told her. "It's time to quit for today anyway."

Lisa nodded reluctantly and did a cartwheel to dismount from the balance beam. As she started for the locker room, Lisa heard a deep voice call, "Lisa! Wait a minute!"

It was Jeff! He left his friend Steve leaning against the back wall of the gym and walked toward her. Lisa could feel her heart beating faster. Had Jeff and Steve been watching her?

Jeff stopped a few steps from her and stuck his hands in his back pockets. "I heard you were going to a big gymnastics meet," he said. "Our swim coach told us." Lisa smiled. All Megan's plans were for nothing! Jeff had found out about the regionals by himself.

"Maybe I'll come and watch you there, too." Jeff's eyes looked into hers. Lisa noticed that they almost matched the blue towel over his shoulder.

"Uh, okay," Lisa mumbled. Suddenly she couldn't think of another thing to say.

"Well, see you Monday in school!" He turned and walked to the back of the gym, where Steve was waiting for him.

Lisa was so excited she felt like doing flips all over the gym, but she forced herself to walk slowly into the locker room with the other girls from her class.

Her friend, Kelly, came up behind her. "I saw you talking to Jeff!" Kelly told her, smiling. "He's so cute! I wish he'd watch me with those blue eyes!"

Lisa grinned at Kelly. I can't wait to go to the regionals, Lisa told herself, especially with Jeff watching.

That night, Lisa dreamed she was watching the Olympics on TV. She was in a thick cast, lying in a hospital bed in their living room. The cast looked a lot like the one her mother wore in the old picture. She woke up the next morning trembling with fear.

Six

WELL, here I am again, Lisa thought, wearing another scratchy paper robe and sitting on another padded table. She watched her mother pace nervously back and forth in the orthopedist's tiny examining room. Lisa had asked her mom to come in with her this time. Now she wasn't sure that had been a good idea.

"Dr. Burns will take X rays today," her mom was telling her. "And he'll measure your legs to make sure they're the same length. At least that's what they did in my day."

If her mother pointed out one more thing that was like when she was young, Lisa was going to scream. I'm not the same as you, she wanted to yell. And I don't have scoliosis!

Finally, Dr. Burns came in. He wasn't very tall, and Lisa noticed that his white coat barely buttoned over his stomach.

"Well, young lady, aren't you missing school this afternoon?" he asked with a smile. Lisa tried to smile, but she was too nervous.

Dr. Burns started by asking her to bend over, just like Dr. O'Neil had. Then he had her stand up and bend to the right and to the left. As he ran his cold fingers down her bare backbone, Lisa decided that all doctors must put their hands in the freezer for a few minutes before they go into examining rooms. Or maybe they carry bags of ice cubes in their coat pockets. Still, she was careful to stand as straight as possible.

"I understand you have scoliosis, too, Mrs. Conklin," Dr. Burns remarked. Lisa noticed her mother hadn't sat down yet. She began to wonder who was more nervous.

"Yes," her mom answered quickly, "but mine wasn't found in time and I had to have surgery. I know Lisa will be different."

That's right! Lisa silently agreed. I don't even have scoliosis in the first place!

Dr. Burns said, "Well, we'll soon know. Just lie back on the table now, Lisa. I want to make sure your legs are the same length." As he measured each leg from hip bone to ankle bone, Lisa glanced over at her mom and smiled a little. Her mom nodded, but didn't smile. Suddenly Lisa realized how worried her mother was. She wanted to tell her everything would be okay. It had to be.

"Well, let's take some X rays," the doctor suggested. "My technician will be right in to get you, Lisa."

As soon as he left, a young woman stuck her head in the door. "Lisa? Come with me," she said.

The X ray machine looked big and scary, but Lisa knew that X rays never hurt. The technician, whose name tag said "Joyce," took more X rays while Lisa stood against a metal screen that had shields on it, and bent this way and that. "Okay, that's it," Joyce said at last. "Go on back to the room with your mother. Dr. Burns will be in as soon as he's seen these."

Lisa held her paper robe together in the back while she walked barefoot back to the examining room. Her mother was sitting by herself in one of the chairs, but she quickly stood up again when Lisa came in.

"All set?" her mom asked.

Lisa nodded. "Dr. Burns will come back in after he looks at my X rays." She felt her hands begin to shake.

Lisa's mother hugged her tight. The paper robe made a crinkly sound. "Whatever happens today, honey, we're in this together," Mrs. Conklin said softly.

Lisa nodded again and hugged her mother back. *Nothing* was going to happen today. It just couldn't.

Just then the door opened. Dr. Burns came in carrying a big, floppy X ray. He smiled at them and attached the X ray to the front of a lighted box that hung on the wall.

That can't be *my* back! Lisa told herself. He must have brought the wrong X ray! She knew that the light-colored shapes down the middle of the X ray were the bones in her spine. They curved slightly to the right in the middle of her chest and then back to the left, just above her waist.

Lisa took deep, slow breaths so she wouldn't faint again. She glanced up at her mother who was standing close beside her. Her mom's lips were pressed tightly together.

"Your back has two curves, in an S shape," Dr. Burns explained. "Right now the curves are about the same—the top one is twenty-eight degrees and the bottom is thirty-one degrees." He pointed at some lines he had drawn on the X rays to measure the curves. "They tend to balance each other out. That's why Lisa still looks like she is standing straight."

Lisa fought back her tears. She couldn't believe that was her back. I not only have scoliosis, she told herself, I've got it bad. This can't be happening to me! Not now!

She tried to talk but her mouth was so dry that no words came out. Finally she whispered, "Do I need an operation?"

"Not at this point, Lisa," Dr. Burns said. "We usually don't operate unless the curve is 45 degrees or more."

Lisa took a deep breath and felt her shoulder muscles start to relax a bit. It's going to be okay, she told herself. I'll be able to go to the regionals.

Then Lisa heard her mom ask "How long would she have to wear it?"

"Wear what?" Lisa asked quickly. A chill went through her body.

"A brace, Lisa, to keep your back from curving more," Dr. Burns told her.

Lisa stared at him. This can't be happening, she told herself. She reached down and gave her leg a hard pinch, but Dr. Burns didn't disappear.

"The brace is made of hard plastic," he explained. "It starts just below your underarms and goes down far enough to cover your hips. It will hold your back as straight as possible and keep your curve from getting worse while you finish growing."

"Finish growing? I'm only thirteen!"

Lisa said. “That will take forever!”

“It will be about three or four years,” he said gently. “We can tell when you’ve stopped growing by taking an X ray of your wrist bones. At that point, you can gradually stop wearing the brace, and your back shouldn’t get any worse than it is right now.”

“But what about the regionals?” She turned to her mother. “I can’t get ready for them in a brace!” Lisa knew she was talking too loudly, but she didn’t care. “It will keep me from bending. My muscles will stiffen up. I’ll lose my flexibility! I’ll lose the regionals!”

“I want you to take the brace off and exercise for twenty minutes or so every day, Lisa, so your muscles won’t get stiff,” Dr. Burns said.

“That’s not enough!” Lisa shouted. Tears rushed to her eyes, and she brushed them away with the backs of her hands.

Mrs. Conklin put her arm around her daughter’s shoulders. Lisa leaned against her and tried to take deep breaths so she wouldn’t cry in front of Dr. Burns.

“Lisa is an excellent gymnast,” her mother explained to the doctor. “She won first place in the state meet this year. She planned to be in a regional competition next month.”

Dr. Burns looked at Lisa for a long moment.

She held her breath. Maybe he would understand how important this was. "Well," he finally said, "you could exercise for up to an hour every day, as long as you wore the brace for the other twenty-three hours."

"An hour?" Lisa couldn't believe it! "I need to practice at least two or three hours a day to be any good for the regionals! In an hour I'd barely be warmed up!"

"Lisa, you need to realize that wearing a brace for too short a period is almost like not wearing it at all," Dr. Burns said softly.

"You don't understand!" she told him in a choked voice. "If I have to wear a brace, I'll have to quit gymnastics!"

Finally, the tears Lisa had been holding back spilled out. The tears dripped off her chin and made soggy spots on the paper robe. Her mother hugged her and said that everything would be all right. But Lisa knew she was wrong. Nothing would be right ever again if she had to quit gymnastics.

Lisa remembered the state meet. When the judges handed her the first-place trophy, flashbulbs went off all around her. Everyone clapped like crazy. Her mother had smiled and cried at the same time. Her dad had had a silly grin on his face. Even Grandma Conklin had come to watch. Lisa remembered seeing her talking to a woman standing near her. She knew Grandma was proudly telling the woman that Lisa was her granddaughter.

And now she'd have to wear a brace! She couldn't go to the regionals. She would never compete again. I don't deserve this, Lisa told herself. I have never done anything bad enough to deserve this!

Dr. Burns handed her some tissues, and Lisa dabbed at her face with them. There has to be a way out of this awful mess, she thought. Then an idea came to her. Maybe, just maybe, the doctor would agree. He had to!

She looked up at Dr. Burns. "What if we wait until after the regionals to get the brace?" she begged. "That's only one more month! If I don't do well at the regionals, I'll drop out of gymnastics. I'll wear the brace twenty-four hours a day. I promise!" She tried to force her mouth into a smile.

"And what if you do well at the regionals?" Dr. Burns asked. "Would you put off getting the brace until after the next competition and maybe until after the one after that?"

Lisa squeezed the damp tissues into a tight ball and stared at the floor. Why can't you understand? she wanted to scream.

"Lisa, any curve that's twenty-five degrees

or more is likely to get worse without treatment," Dr. Burns told her. "Some doctors wait until a curve measures thirty degrees to begin treatment, but they would treat you, too. Curves like yours, especially with a history of scoliosis in the family, can progress ten degrees in just a few months."

Lisa closed her eyes. He can't be talking about me, she thought desperately. I am strong and healthy! I am a gymnast!

"With the amount of growing you have ahead of you, a thirty-degree curve could, without treatment, progress to forty-five degrees or more. At that point a brace won't help," Dr. Burns explained. "Then we would have to operate. In a few cases, a brace doesn't stop the curve from progressing and we have to operate anyway. Then we put metal rods beside the spinal column to stabilize it. That part of the person's back never bends again."

Lisa shook her head. "But nothing hurts!" she insisted. "I'm not sick and I don't need a brace to make me better!"

"Lisa, I can already see beginning symptoms of your scoliosis without an X ray," Dr. Burns told her. "Your right shoulder is slightly higher than the left. Your right hip is a little higher, too. Haven't you noticed that your skirts and dresses are shorter on one side than the other?"

Some of my dresses do look lopsided, Lisa realized. I thought they were just made wrong.

"Your right shoulder blade sticks out just a little, too," he added.

Lisa looked at him angrily. Her eyes burned from crying. "I'll bet you're the only one in the world who would notice the difference in my shoulders and hips!"

"You may be right, today. But in a year or two, you might have trouble finding clothes that hide the problem," he told her.

"Lisa, we can handle this together," her mother promised. "At least at this point you don't need surgery."

"Wearing a brace will be almost as bad!"

Lisa insisted. She felt her eyes fill again with hot tears. "I'll have to quit gymnastics! It's all I care about! I might have been in the Olympics! And now," she said between sobs, "I'll never know! I'll never know!"

Seven

BY the time Lisa and her mom got home, it was already after five o'clock. Mr. Conklin met them at the door. "What did the doctor say?" he asked.

"I have to wear a brace! For three or four years!" Lisa told him. "I have to quit gymnastics!"

Lisa saw the shocked look on her father's face. Suddenly she couldn't stand to talk about it anymore. She ran up the stairs to her room and slammed the door. She rolled into a ball on her bed and cried some more. Finally, she stopped crying and lay exhausted and hiccupping.

As she lay there, she heard her parents arguing downstairs. Lisa got up and slowly opened her bedroom door. As she did, she caught a glimpse of her red, blotchy face in her dresser mirror. I look about as bad as

I feel, she thought to herself.

Lisa crept to the top of the stairs and sat down.

"We have to get a second opinion," her father was saying. "Before we do anything, we have to ask another doctor. Maybe there's a better way to handle this."

"Dr. Burns specializes in scoliosis, George," Mrs. Conklin reminded him. "I really think he knows what he's doing!"

"Gymnastics are Lisa's life!" her father insisted.

"And your life, too, right?" her mom asked.

Her father didn't answer right away. She imagined him staring angrily at her mother. Then he said, "I just want to make sure she absolutely has to quit. She's so good, so darn good! My boss even planned to come and watch her at the regionals. He was going to bring his video-recorder so he could tape her for us. He doesn't have any kids of his own. He said this was the closest he would get to a real champion."

Lisa felt even more tears coming. She put her hand over her mouth so her parents wouldn't hear her cry. The tears ran over her fingers.

No one spoke downstairs for a minute. Then her mother said, "I guess one more opinion wouldn't hurt." Her voice was so low Lisa could hardly hear her.

"We'll call another doctor first thing tomorrow morning," her father quickly agreed.

"As soon as we get an appointment, I'll rearrange my schedule so I can go with you this time."

"What about Lisa's lesson at the gym?" her mother asked. "Today's Monday. It's almost time for it."

Silence again. Then her mother spoke.

"Why don't I call and explain the situation to Mrs. Pogue?" she suggested.

"Wait, Ann," Mr. Conklin said. "Let's not say anything to anyone until we get a second opinion. I'll call and say Lisa's sick tonight. She's already had a hard day anyway."

"George . . . ," her mother objected.

"Just this once, Ann," he said. "It won't hurt anything to wait a few more days before we talk to Mrs. Pogue. Let's be sure before we make any big decisions. This is too important to Lisa!"

Mrs. Conklin said nothing. Instead, Lisa heard her go into the kitchen, where she made a lot of noise getting dinner ready.

Lisa moved quietly back to her room and softly closed her door again. She had fallen asleep on the bed by the time her mother came up to tell her dinner was ready.

"I'm not hungry, Mom," Lisa told her sleepily. She was surprised to see that it was already dark outside.

"You really should eat, honey."

"Not tonight, Mom. I really don't feel well," Lisa told her.

Her mom sat on her bed in the darkness. She brushed Lisa's hair back from her face. Tears had stuck strands of it to her cheeks.

"I know what will happen if I start wearing a brace," Lisa said quietly. "Quitting gymnastics is only the beginning." She sighed. "The kids at school will find out about the brace, and they'll think I'm not normal."

"Not your friends, Lisa," her mother said. "They already know what a great girl you are. A brace won't change that."

"But I don't have a boyfriend, and I'll never get one if I have to wear a brace! No boy wants to go with a girl everyone feels sorry for!" She swallowed hard, thinking about Jeff.

Mrs. Conklin took her daughter's hand. "Wearing a brace isn't going to be easy, honey, but it really could be worse. I remember the day I left seventh grade to go into the hospital for my surgery. I was standing in the hall talking with both of my teachers. I only had two. It was the Dark Ages, you know."

Lisa smiled in spite of herself.

"I was crying and they were trying to convince me everything would be all right. I didn't believe them, of course. I was sure it was the end of my life." The moonlight from the window was shining on her mother's face. Lisa could see lines under her eyes.

Mrs. Conklin sighed. "I guess it was easier for me because I never was very athletic, but there were still problems. After the operation I stayed in bed in that heavy cast for the last month of seventh grade, the whole summer, and about three months of eighth grade."

"You missed all that school?" Lisa asked.

Her mom smiled and shook her head. "A tutor came to our house for an hour a day to help me keep up with my school work. Finally, the doctor cut me out of the cast. Then I was fitted for a hard plastic brace, something like the one you'll wear. The first day I went back to school . . . ," She paused.

"What happened?" Lisa asked softly. Her mother had never mentioned any of this before.

"The first day I went back, one of the most popular girls in my class looked at me and said, 'Oh, you were gone so long, I forgot about you.' That wasn't exactly the welcome I had hoped for."

Lisa wished she could punch whoever said that to her mother. She sat up and hugged her.

"In spite of everything," her mom went on, "those months were a tiny part of my life. I am very glad my parents made sure I had the treatment I needed, whether I wanted it or not. Without it, I would look very different now. I'd be twisted and hunched over. And I'd be in pain."

Lisa leaned against her mother's shoulder. She and Megan had often talked about how they would look when they were older, but Lisa had never for a minute thought she would be twisted and hunched over.

This can't be happening to me! she told herself again.

"I'm tired now, Mom," Lisa said. I just want to be alone. I especially don't want to hear any more about my back or my mother's back. Maybe when I wake up in the morning this will all be a bad dream.

Eight

LISA and Megan sat next to each other at lunch the next day, just like they always did. Megan was worried. Their math class was right after lunch, and she hadn't done her homework, again.

"Help me think of a good excuse, Lisa," Megan begged. "The teacher didn't believe me the last time when I told him someone took my book."

"Maybe that's because you had your book right in front of you," Lisa suggested. She ate a corner off her peanut butter sandwich.

"Lisa, I had to take my book to class," Megan insisted. "You know the teachers take points off if you don't have your book!"

Lisa shook her head. "Oh, Megan," she said with an exasperated smile.

She watched Megan hunt through her lunch bag for her cookies. They had shared sweaters and candy bars and movies and secrets ever since fourth grade. Now I have another secret for you, Lisa thought, an important one. Maybe Dad doesn't want anyone to know yet, but I've got to talk to somebody.

"I went to an orthopedist yesterday," Lisa said quietly.

"You did?" Megan immediately stopped looking for her cookies. "Isn't that some kind of doctor?"

Lisa nodded. "They think I have scoliosis," Lisa said, feeling her voice grow hoarse. I might have to wear a brace for three or four years."

"Well, that won't be too bad," Megan said. "Lots of kids wear braces. Remember when I wore them?" Lisa sighed impatiently. "Not braces on my teeth!" Lisa told her. "A brace for my back, from here to here." She held one hand level with her underarm and the other at the top of her leg.

"A brace for your back?" Megan repeated. "Why do you need a brace like that?" She was beginning to look worried.

"They say my back is growing crooked," Lisa told her. "The brace is supposed to keep it from getting worse."

Megan tipped her chair back so that she

could see Lisa's sweater-covered back. Then she frowned. "You look fine to me, Lisa. Why does the doctor think your back is growing crooked?"

"He looked at my back and took X rays. He said one of my shoulders is higher than the other. One hip, too," Lisa answered.

Megan stared at Lisa's shoulders for a second. "Look at my shoulders, Lisa. Do they look okay to you?" Megan asked. She sat up straight and stiff.

Suddenly, Lisa had an irresistible urge to tease Megan.

"Well, Megan," Lisa began, "your left shoulder does look a little higher than your right one, now that I think about it."

"It does?" Megan whispered. "Do you think I caught it from you?"

Megan looked so scared that Lisa smiled. "Megan, I'm kidding! And anyway, you can't catch scoliosis from another person." She told her friend what she knew about it.

Megan thought for a minute. "At least you don't have to be in a cast, like your mom in that picture."

"But I might not get to go to the regionals! I'll have to give up gymnastics!" Lisa said in a rush. "I've worked so hard! The only reason Jeff talked to me was because he thought I was going to the regionals."

Lisa sighed. "My dad is really proud of my gymnastics," she said softly. "Sometimes I think he would have been happier if I had been a boy. He's going to be awfully disappointed if I have to quit gymnastics."

"Lisa, I'm always going to be your best friend—brace or no brace," Megan said with a reassuring smile. "You can still go to the movies with a brace on, can't you?"

Lisa nodded and smiled weakly.

Megan found her cookies in her lunch bag and gave one to Lisa. Lisa ate it slowly while she watched kids shuffle past their table toward the cafeteria door.

Suddenly something shiny caught her eye. Someone—a boy—was wearing a metal brace on one leg. She could see a couple of inches of it between the bottom of his jeans and his shoe.

Lisa looked up. It was Steve! Her eyes moved from his face to the brace and back again as he stood near her, waiting for a crowd of kids to move out of the way.

"Hi, Lisa," Steve said. Oh, no! Lisa thought. He saw me staring at his brace!

"Uh, hi, Steve." Lisa didn't know what to say. She tried not to look at the brace again. "Uh, I . . . I didn't know that was you! I mean,

I didn't notice your brace—your leg, I mean—before. I didn't expect . . . " Lisa felt her face start to burn.

Steve opened his mouth to say something, but Lisa kept talking. "I was just surprised! I'm . . . I didn't . . . " *I'm making it worse!* Lisa told herself in panic. She grabbed her books and shoved through the crowd out the cafeteria door.

What's wrong with me? Lisa asked herself a minute later as she hid in a stall in the girls' restroom. *Poor Steve! I just made sure everyone in the cafeteria knew he was wearing a brace!*

Lisa leaned against the cool metal wall. *What a mess!* she thought miserably. *I wouldn't blame Megan if she pretends she doesn't know me. Steve will probably tell Jeff what a jerk I am. Then neither one of them will ever talk to me again!*

Maybe my parents will let me transfer to another school and start over. Maybe I could start my whole life over!

Lisa spent the rest of the school day avoiding Megan. After dinner that night, Lisa heard the phone ring downstairs, even with her bedroom door closed. *It must be Megan,* she guessed. *She's calling to tell me how much I embarrassed her today, just when she was* trying to impress Steve. Lisa thought about pretending she was asleep, but it was only seven o'clock.

"Lisa! Megan's on the phone!" her mother called up the stairs.

I know—I'll run to the bathroom and turn on the shower, Lisa thought. I can't answer the phone when I'm taking a shower, right? But it is too late for that. I have to face her sooner or later, Lisa decided, unless I could talk Mom and Dad into moving to another town. She opened her door and yelled, "I'll get it, Mom!"

Lisa picked up the phone in her parents' bedroom. "Megan, before you say anything, I'm sorry! I really am! I know I embarrassed you today!"

"Lisa, Steve—" Megan began.

"Oh, I know how much you like him," Lisa interrupted. "I'll write him a note and apologize. I'll tell him you and I barely know each other!"

Megan tried again. "But I told Steve—"

"I don't blame you for anything you told him! I can't believe I ran out and left you there. Please don't be too mad!"

"Lisa! Let me talk!" Megan yelled over the phone. "Steve asked me out!"

"What?" That was the last thing Lisa expected to hear!

"After you left," Megan explained, "I told Steve that you might have to wear a brace and that's why you were surprised to see that he wore one, too. All he said was 'Oh.' He wasn't embarrassed at all!"

"He wasn't?"

"No! Steve told me he's worn that brace on his leg for a couple of years," Megan said, "ever since a car hit him while he was riding his bike. His leg was broken and a nerve in it was hurt somehow. Now when he doesn't wear the brace, his foot shakes. Steve said he's glad to have the brace."

"But Steve is on the swim team," Lisa said. "How can he swim with a brace on?"

"He doesn't! He takes it off while he swims," Megan explained impatiently. "But this is the best part! Steve asked me to go bowling with him this Saturday! His parents bowl in a league, and we're going with them. We'll bowl by ourselves, though. He said he would teach me how!" She giggled. "It'll be my first date!"

Lisa didn't know what to say. "That's great, Megan," she finally managed. "I'm really glad I didn't embarrass Steve." She twisted the phone cord around her finger. "I guess you and I won't be going to the movies this Saturday."

Megan didn't answer at first. "Oh, Lisa, I'm

sorry. I forgot. I'll go with you next week, okay?"

Lisa was so glad that Megan was still her friend, she almost didn't mind missing the movies for one week. "It's okay, Megan, if you promise to tell me everything that happens. And find out if Jeff is going with anyone, will you?" Not that it will do me any good to know, Lisa told herself.

"Sure! One other thing, Lisa. Could I borrow your blouse, the one with the wild pattern down the front?" Megan asked. "My chest exercises haven't started to work yet, but I read in a magazine that patterns make your chest look bigger!"

Lisa smiled. "Sure, Megan." Suddenly Lisa felt very tired. "I'll see you at lunch tomorrow. Oh, wait a minute! My dad made an appointment with another orthopedist tomorrow at eleven-thirty. He said the doctor had a cancellation then. I'll probably miss lunch at school."

"Oh, okay. I'll be thinking about you," Megan said. "Good luck!"

"Thanks, Meg." After Lisa hung up, she walked back to her room and sat on her bed. The balance beam still stretched across her floor. She kicked it.

Megan has a date, Lisa thought, a real date. What if she and Steve start going together? What if she starts eating lunch with him every day?

My life has turned into a nightmare, Lisa told herself. Maybe if I cross all my fingers and all my toes, the doctor we see tomorrow will say this was all a mistake. He'll say I'm the strongest, healthiest girl he's seen in a long time. I'll stay in gymnastics, and Jeff and my dad will both be watching when I take first place in the regionals! After all, nothing hurts. Nothing hurts but my heart.

Nine

BY twenty minutes after eleven the next morning, Lisa and her parents were sitting in hard plastic chairs in Dr. Killinger's waiting room. Lisa glanced at her mom sitting beside her. Mrs. Conklin seemed to be reading a book, but Lisa noticed she hadn't turned a page yet.

Her dad shifted restlessly in the chair on the other side of Lisa. Every once in a while he smiled at her. He was holding a giant envelope containing her X rays from Dr. Burns's office. They had brought them here so Dr. Killinger wouldn't have to take more.

Lisa pictured Dr. Killinger dipping his hands in ice water so he would be ready to run his fingers down her backbone.

Lisa had just started reading the same magazine article for the third time when an older woman hobbled into the waiting room.

At first Lisa thought the woman's right leg was much shorter than her left one. Her whole body moved down when she stood on her right leg and up when she stood on her left leg. Then Lisa realized that the woman's right hip was much higher than her left one, making it seem as if her legs were different lengths.

The woman's loose jacket doesn't hide her shoulder either, Lisa noticed. Her right shoulder was twisted up almost to her ear. And her right shoulder blade stuck out and made a hump on her back. Lisa guessed the woman wasn't any taller than she was. Lisa watched as she carefully eased herself into a chair across from the Conklins. A little boy sitting beside his mother in the waiting room stared at her.

Lisa felt her face getting hot. She looked down at the magazine she was still holding, but she couldn't see the words. I know what's wrong with her, she thought. She has scoliosis. This is what can happen. Suddenly Lisa had a sick feeling in her stomach. She had to swallow to keep from throwing up.

Lisa looked at her father. He was staring at the X ray envelope in his lap, but his face was pale. Lisa heard him take two deep breaths. He reached over and took her hand without looking at her.

"Lisa Conklin?" It was that time again. As they all started to get up, Lisa realized that her father and mother were coming with her. I really don't need this, she told herself.

"Let me go in by myself, okay?" she asked her parents, trying to keep her voice from shaking. "After he checks my back, you both can come in and talk to him."

"All right, honey," her mother said. Her dad nodded quickly, and they both sat down again.

A little later in the examining room, Lisa sat wearing still another paper robe. This one was light blue. A forest of trees must have died so I could wear all these paper robes, she decided.

Dr. Killinger stood nearby, carefully tracing her backbone down the X ray from Dr. Burns. His gray hair made a kind of halo around his head. It matched his mustache.

If I don't ask now, Lisa decided, I'll never know.

"I . . . I saw a lady in the waiting room who must have scoliosis, too," Lisa began. "It looked like . . . like it was too late to help her." Lisa felt her eyes getting hot. Oh, please, she told herself. No more tears.

"Mmmm. I think I know who you're talking about," Dr. Killinger said. "That woman's curvature probably wasn't any worse than yours,

Lisa, when she was your age, but hers wasn't detected, and it wasn't treated. She told me her mother just kept telling her to stand up straight."

. . . probably wasn't any worse than yours . . ., Lisa thought. That's what I was afraid you were going to say.

Dr. Killinger sat on a stool and motioned for Lisa to stand in front of him. "Because her body is so far off-balance, her curve is still getting about one degree worse every year," he remarked. "That may not sound like much, but it means that now her curve is about 25 degrees worse than when she was a teenager."

He inched his fingers down both sides of Lisa's spine as he talked. "The vertebrae in that woman's backbone are so far out of line that soon they won't be able to support her weight. She won't be able to walk or stand. She's already having trouble breathing because her ribs are pressing on her chest cavity. She's had back pain for years, and it's getting worse."

Lisa remembered how slowly the woman moved. "Is it hopeless?" she asked in a small voice.

"Not at all," Dr. Killinger told her. "We're planning surgery for her. We'll put a steel rod in her back and wire her vertebrae to it. The rod and wires will hold her spine straighter.

She probably won't even need a cast after the operation. She will lose some of the bending and twisting of her back where we've joined the vertebrae together, but she can't move very well now either."

"Will her back be perfectly straight?" Lisa asked. She hoped so. The woman had smiled at her when she walked past. She looked almost normal, sitting down.

"No, we can't make it perfectly straight," Dr. Killinger answered. "When your spine has been curved like that for so long, the vertebrae and muscles change shape a little to accommodate the curve. It's nearly impossible to make them completely straight again. Her back will be much straighter, though, and she'll probably be several inches taller. The most important thing is, her curve won't get worse."

She'll look a lot better, too, Lisa thought. Suddenly she wished she could talk to the woman. She wanted to wish her good luck on her surgery.

Dr. Killinger stood up. "Well, Dr. Burns was right about your back," he said. "Why don't you get dressed and we'll talk to your parents in my office?"

Lisa and her parents sat in Dr. Killinger's office while the doctor answered their questions. Then he had a question of his own.

"Dr. Burns's note said Lisa's scoliosis was diagnosed during a routine physical. Didn't the school nurse find it when she did her scoliosis screening?"

"I don't think they do scoliosis screenings at the middle school," Lisa's mom answered. "Sometimes they do it and sometimes they don't. I guess they . . . missed Lisa."

He shook his head. "This state still doesn't have a law to require screening. Half the states do." He looked at Lisa. "It's so important to catch this early, so that we don't have to do surgery."

Lisa stared at her hands in her lap. Her fingernails were stubby and broken where she had chewed on them, but she didn't care.

"If you don't have any more questions," the doctor said, "I suggest you follow Dr. Burns's recommendation. The sooner Lisa gets her brace, the better."

Dr. Killinger shook hands with Mr. and Mrs. Conklin and left to see another patient. Lisa and her parents sat for a minute without moving or talking. Then Lisa's father turned to her and took her hand. He didn't smile. Lisa knew she didn't want to hear what he was going to say. She remembered the last time she had seen him look so sad. It had been last year at her grandfather's funeral.

"Well, Lisa, I guess you know what we have to do," he said in a hoarse voice. "No one ever said life was fair."

Lisa stared at him for a second. She turned to her mother, but Mrs. Conklin just nodded slightly.

This is it, then, she thought. I have to wear a brace for four years. No regionals, no picture in the paper, no more gymnastics. Grandma will have to tell her friends about her granddaughter with the handicap instead of her granddaughter the top gymnast. I'll never even know if I'm good enough for the Olympics. She remembered how excited her father had been at the state meet. Lisa closed her eyes to try to keep her tears in.

Her dad squeezed her hand. "I'll go with you tonight to talk to Mrs. Pogue," he said. "She'll be disappointed. I think you are her favorite, probably the best gymnast she ever coached."

Lisa's chin started to quiver. She brushed her tears away with the back of her hand.

"We'll face this together, though." He reached across Lisa and took his wife's hand, too. Lisa saw how they looked at each other. Lisa wondered if anyone would ever love her as much as her parents loved each other.

"Tomorrow, let's call that specialist who

makes braces," her father suggested. "What did Dr. Burns call him?"

"An orthotist," his wife said. Lisa thought her mother's voice sounded kind of raw, as if she had a cold.

"I'll go with you to get the brace fitted, if you want, Lisa," her father offered. "I certainly don't have anything more important to do."

Lisa thought for a second. "That's okay, Dad," she said. "Just Mom and I can go. She's been through this all before, anyway." Lisa looked at her mother. A tear slipped down her mom's cheek, right past her smile.

When her parents drove her back to school, Lisa sat in the front, between them, the way she used to when she was younger. It was crowded, but somehow it made her feel better.

While her parents talked about insurance and appointments, Lisa wondered how it would feel to wear a brace. Will all the kids at school know? she wondered. Will they think I'm handicapped now? Maybe somebody will think I should go to a special class. Will they know I'm still the same person, only I have a problem with my back? What will Jeff think, if he ever thinks about me at all?

Ten

LISA didn't see Megan the rest of the school day, but right after school Megan called to find out what the second doctor said.

"He said the same thing as the one before. I need a brace," Lisa told her in a wooden voice. "Mom already made an appointment to get one next Monday."

"Oh, that's too bad," Megan said softly. "Monday," she repeated. "Well, how about some good news?"

"Sure," Lisa said glumly.

"I was talking to Steve at lunch time and . . . ," Megan began.

Lisa felt her heart sink. I knew this would happen, she told herself. Megan will eat lunch with Steve every day. I wonder if Kelly and Ann from my gymnastics class would let me eat lunch with them from now on.

"Jeff was there, too. He was looking for you

because he wanted to ask you to go bowling with us on Saturday!" Megan said without taking a breath.

"Jeff wants me to go? Didn't Steve tell him what I said in the cafeteria yesterday?" Lisa couldn't believe her ears.

"I told you Steve wasn't embarrassed by that!" Megan insisted. "I bet he didn't even mention it to Jeff. Jeff wants you to come. I do, too! Just think! It'll be our very first date, and we'll be together!"

It does sound like fun, Lisa thought. At least I'll have one date with Jeff before I have to wear that brace.

"I have to ask my parents," she told Megan. "They'll probably say it's okay if you're coming, too, and Steve's parents will be there. But Meg, are you sure Steve isn't mad at me?"

"Don't worry about it, Lisa!"

A little later, as Lisa was trying to remember whether she had any homework, her dad called up the stairs. "Time to go to the gym, Lisa!"

"But, Dad, I'm not . . . " Then Lisa remembered that they still had to tell Mrs. Pogue.

As soon as Mrs. Pogue saw Lisa in her jeans instead of workout clothes, she frowned. The frown never left her face as Mr. Conklin told her about the scoliosis.

Lisa tried not to listen. She watched a girl from her class practicing handstands on the balance beam. Over in the corner of the gym Ann was going through some floor exercises to music from a boom box. Lisa recognized the song. It was one she had used, too.

Several of the girls waved to her. Lisa waved back, but she didn't walk over to talk to anyone. She didn't want to do anymore explaining right now.

Two of the younger girls from Mrs. Pogue's beginners class edged up to Lisa and shyly asked if she were going to practice tonight. Lisa smiled and shook her head. She hoped her face didn't look as sad as she felt.

Kelly was practicing dismounts on the uneven bars. Lisa remembered the blisters she had gotten on her hands the first time she tried the bars. She wished she could take one more turn.

Her father stopped talking. Mrs. Pogue put her arm around Lisa's shoulders and looked into her eyes. She slowly shook her head. "Lisa, I'm really sorry. I feel as if I should have known."

Lisa swallowed. "It's okay, Mrs. Pogue. You couldn't have changed anything anyway." Lisa looked at the floor so they couldn't see the tears in her eyes. "I'm . . . I'm really glad you were my coach. I . . . I really liked gymnastics."

No one spoke. Lisa's nose started running. Without thinking, she wiped it on her coat sleeve.

"Maybe you can't be in the regionals, Lisa," her father said finally, "but I'm sure you can come and go through your routines for an hour a day. Dr. Burns said you needed to keep exercising, remember?"

"Come to think of it, Lisa, I really could use your help," Mrs. Pogue told her.

Lisa looked up in surprise.

"The girls in the beginner's class think you're the best gymnast ever!" her coach said. Her gray eyes were still serious, but the corners of her mouth turned up in a little smile. "Could you help me with their class? It would keep you limber and it would really help me out. They would think they were in heaven!"

Lisa didn't trust her voice to talk. "I'll think about it," she finally said. But to herself she thought, I don't think I'll ever come back here. It just wouldn't be the same.

As Lisa slowly followed her father out of the gym, they passed the pool. The door was closed, but Lisa could hear splashes and the coach's whistle. She knew that Jeff was in there. She suddenly remembered that her very first date was only two days away. At least that's one thing to look forward to, she told herself.

Then another thought came: I don't even know what you're supposed to do on a date! But I guess it's really not a big problem, Lisa decided. After I get the brace, no one will ask me out again. Saturday will be my first and last date, ever.

Eleven

LISA was glad it was Steve's turn to bowl first. That way I can get a good look at his brace and he won't even know it, she told herself. Lisa sat with Megan, Steve, and Jeff in the circle of seats around the scoring table. She could hear Steve's parents and the other adults in their bowling league laughing and talking a few lanes down.

Steve walked to the center of the lane and stood holding the ball in front of him for a few seconds as he stared at the pins. He squinted in concentration. Steve was wearing bowling shoes, just like everyone else. Megan had told Lisa that Steve's leg brace didn't attach to his shoe. It started just below his knee and had two metal strips that went down each side of his leg to his foot. The strips attached to a plastic piece that had been molded to fit the sides and bottom of Steve's foot. The plastic piece slipped inside Steve's shoe.

Steve lifted the ball, swung it backward, took several steps, and smoothly sent the ball speeding toward the pins. He left two standing, but he knocked them down with the second ball. Steve turned and grinned at Lisa and Megan.

Lisa glanced around, but no one seemed to be paying any attention to Steve's brace. Jeff had gone up to the snack bar for snacks and Megan . . . . well, I can see Megan isn't worried about Steve's brace, Lisa thought. Megan, wearing Lisa's blouse, was smiling up at Steve as he told her how to write his score on the scoresheet.

"I usually get a strike," Steve bragged to her, "but we've had swim meets the last three weekends in a row. I'm out of practice!" Megan nodded and smiled again.

"Swim meets?" Lisa asked. She turned to Jeff and almost spilled the drink he was handing her. "Do you compete against other teams?"

Jeff laughed. "Well, kind of," he told her. "Actually, we just go to make the other teams look good. Remember two weeks ago, Steve, at Granville? It's a good thing we didn't swim against their girls' team. They would have beat us, too!"

Steve laughed and shook his head.

“You must feel bad when you lose,” Lisa remarked. She remembered last year, when she had come in fourth at the state gymnastic meet. She hadn’t said a word during the whole two-hour drive home in the car.

“Feel bad?” Jeff repeated. “Why? We’re just having fun.”

“It sounds like fun to me!” Megan said. “What do you have to do to get on the team?”

Lisa tried not to look surprised. Megan wants to be on the swim team? she asked herself. She wondered if Megan knew that the girls on the swim team don’t just stand around wearing bathing suits. They actually go in the water! The two friends had gone to the pool in the summer hundreds of times, but Lisa had never seen Megan get wet!

Lisa glanced at the scoresheet and suddenly she understood. It was Megan’s turn to bowl next! Lisa smiled to herself. Megan was trying to keep them talking so she wouldn’t have to bowl!

“Never mind the swim team, Meg. It’s your turn to bowl,” Steve told her. “Come on, I’ll help you!”

Steve got up and started toward the rack of balls. Megan gave Lisa a quick look that said “Oh, no!” and slowly followed him. I’m glad Dad takes me bowling sometimes, Lisa thought. At least I know which fingers to put in the holes!

Jeff leaned closer to Lisa. "Hasn't Megan ever been bowling before?" he asked.

Jeff's closeness made Lisa's heart beat faster. "Well, Megan's not much of an athlete," she told him. Except for her chest exercises, Lisa wanted to add, but she just smiled instead.

"Ouch!" Megan yelled. She was frantically shaking her right hand. "My finger got squashed between the balls!" Megan said between gasps of pain. "I think it's broken!"

Lisa and Jeff hurried over. Steve was trying to hold Megan's hand still so he could look at it. All Lisa could see was a flash of red nail polish.

"Let's ask my mom to take a look," Steve suggested. "She's a nurse."

Lisa watched Steve and Megan hurry down three lanes to Steve's parents. She had seen too many of Megan's "broken" bones to be really worried. Suddenly she realized she was alone with Jeff. He sat down at the scoring table again. Lisa sat down next to him.

"Megan'll be okay, I think," Jeff said.

Lisa nodded. Then she couldn't think of anything to say.

Jeff doodled on the scoresheet for a few minutes. "Uh, when is that big gymnastic meet the coach told us about?" he asked. "Is it okay if Steve and I come and watch?"

Lisa looked away to hide her surprise. He doesn't know about my brace! she told herself. Steve must not have told him about that day in the cafeteria after all!

"Uh . . . ," Lisa mumbled. What can I say? she thought. I wish I didn't have to tell him!

"If you don't want me there, it's okay," Jeff said quietly. "Maybe you already asked someone else to come."

"I'm not going!" Lisa blurted out.

Now Jeff looked surprised.

"I have a . . . a physical problem," she said. "I can't go."

Jeff quickly looked down at his hands. He looked embarrassed. "That's too bad," he said.

Since she'd gotten this far, she figured she might as well keep going. "I have scoliosis. I have to start wearing a brace so I can't be in gymnastics anymore." There, she thought, I said it. Everyone in the world might as well know. They'll all find out anyway when I show up at school in a big, ugly brace.

"Scoliosis?" he asked. He looked really confused. "Isn't that a skin disease?"

"No! You don't wear a brace for a skin disease!" Suddenly Lisa wished she hadn't told him after all.

"Okay, I give up," he said. He smiled and shrugged his shoulders. "What is scoliosis?"

Why doesn't he take this more seriously? she thought. "It means my back is starting to grow crooked," Lisa told him. "I have to wear a brace to hold it straight until I finish growing."

Jeff thought for a minute. "And you have to give up gymnastics?" he asked. "Before the big meet?"

Lisa nodded slowly and sighed. "I'm going to get the brace next week."

Jeff shook his head. "It must be hard for you to quit gymnastics," he said. "I sure wouldn't want someone to tell me I couldn't swim anymore and I'm not nearly as good at swimming as you are at gymnastics."

Even though Jeff's words sounded awkward, Lisa thought he probably understood a little. But he probably doesn't understand enough to go out with a girl with a brace.

"That reminds me," Jeff said. "Our swim team is having a party at the pool next Friday. Want to come?"

Lisa just stared at him. Hadn't he heard what she said? Jeff was one of the most popular boys in her class. She'd probably have her brace by then. She might not have to wear it at the pool, but she'd have to wear it before *and* afterward. Jeff would be embarrassed to be seen with her. He was probably just being nice. Well, I'll save him the trouble, Lisa thought.

"Steve is going to ask Megan, too," Jeff added. "I know how you two like to stick together!" He smiled.

"I can't go," she told him. "I'm busy next Friday." You can ask someone else, she wanted to yell, someone who won't embarrass you in front of your friends.

Twelve

WHEN Lisa walked in the door after school on Monday, her mom was waiting to take her to the orthotist's office. "This will only take a minute, honey," she promised. "All he's going to do is measure you so he can order the brace."

We might as well get this over with, Lisa thought. If I stay home, I'll just sit in my bedroom thinking about the gymnastics lesson I'm missing. Megan will probably call and I'll have to explain, again, that I just don't feel like going to the swim team party with Jeff

Why couldn't Megan just go with Steve and stop bugging me? Jeff hardly talked to me Saturday after I told him I couldn't go to his swim party. But the date had started out fun, Lisa thought. I really do like Jeff. I like him enough to make it easy on him and bow out of Friday night's party.

The orthotist was right down the hall from Dr. Burns's office. For once, Lisa didn't have to wear one of the paper robes. Instead, her mother pulled a long undershirt out of her purse. "Take off your sweater and jeans and put this on, Lisa," she said. "When I called for this appointment, the woman asked me to bring it for you to wear."

The undershirt had no sleeves and a scooped neckline, kind of like one her father would wear, except this one was light pink. When Lisa pulled it on, she saw that it was a little tight and just long enough to cover her underpants. It looked a little like a bathing suit.

The orthotist came in. He was tall and thin, with hair the color of sand. His light-colored glasses almost blended in with his face. The name tag on his white coat said "Chris," and he had a measuring tape hanging over one shoulder.

He smiled at Lisa. "Great! You're all ready. If you wear an undershirt like this one under your brace all the time, you'll be more comfortable.

Lisa tried to smile back, just to be polite, but her heart wasn't in it. Chris started measuring her hips, waist, and "development," as Lisa read on the form he was filling out.

"Development," it turned out, meant he measured her chest just below her bust. Lisa closed her eyes and pretended she was someplace else.

"There are basically two ways to make these braces," Chris explained to Lisa's mother.

"We are going to order one that's already made to fit Lisa's measurements. Other orthotists make a plaster mold of the person's body and then have the brace custom-made from the mold. That's more expensive, though, especially when some kids outgrow their first brace and need another one made after a year or two. Dr. Burns thinks our ready-made braces fit just as well, and they don't cost as much."

It doesn't really matter, Lisa wanted to tell him. Either way, a brace is going to make me look weird.

Chris draped the tape measure over his shoulder again and smiled. "That's it for today. Before you go, though, maybe you'd like to see what the brace will look like."

Lisa did not want to know, but she looked at the catalog he was showing them anyway. He pointed to a picture of a white plastic brace that would cover someone's body from just under the arms to the top of the legs. The back was slit open all the way down, so you could take it off, Lisa guessed. There were two buckles across the back to fasten it shut. She wished for the thousandth time that she had never heard of scoliosis.

"Your brace will probably be here Thursday. We'll call you if it gets here before that," Chris told them.

There's no hurry, Lisa thought. I just know I could keep on living without this brace. Then she remembered the woman in Dr. Killinger's waiting room, and her stomach started to ache. She took a deep breath.

By dinnertime Lisa's stomach hurt so badly she couldn't eat. By Tuesday morning she convinced her mother that she was too sick to go to school. Her mother stayed home with her, and all Lisa did was lie in bed under her thick blanket. It was the safest place she could think of. Nothing bad will happen if I stay here, she told herself. She got up once, to grab her big white teddy bear off her dresser. Then she got back under the warm covers and fell asleep hugging him.

Later, when her dad came home, she heard him asking about her. It's rotten to be an only child, she decided. They need someone else to fuss over. Still, Lisa crept out of bed and sat on the top step again.

"I think she really is sick," her mother was insisting.

"She's got to face this, Ann. She can't keep hiding in her bedroom. Tomorrow she goes back to school," her father said.

I am really sick! Lisa wanted to yell down the stairs. There are all kinds of sick, you know! But she didn't want them to know she was listening, so she just got back in bed and pulled the covers up to her neck.

When Megan called, Lisa told her mother she was too sick to talk on the phone. I bet Megan just wants to talk about Steve and the swim party anyway, Lisa grumbled to herself She probably didn't even notice I wasn't in school today.

Lisa didn't feel any better by Wednesday, but her mother wouldn't let her stay home again. Just walking to school wore her out. Her books felt like they weighed ten pounds a piece. When she got to school, she decided to leave her science book in her locker. She just couldn't carry all of her books. In science class the teacher took two points off her grade for not having her book. But she didn't care. She didn't really care about anything.

Then it was lunchtime. But when Lisa walked into the cafeteria to eat lunch with Megan, Steve was already sitting at their table with his lunch spread out! Steve must have told a very funny joke because Megan was laughing her head off I can see how much my best friend misses me! Lisa thought.

She sat down several tables away, with Kelly and Ann from her gymnastics class. That didn't work out either, because Kelly wanted to know why Lisa wasn't at the gym on Monday. Lisa just shrugged her shoulders. There are a lot of nosy people at this school, she told herself.

Jeff stopped her in the hallway after lunch. "I heard you were sick," he said. He put his hand on her arm, as if he wanted her to stop and talk.

"I'm okay," she mumbled. She kept walking. Lisa knew he didn't want to hear about her problems. All she could think of was tomorrow. Tomorrow was the day she would get her brace and begin her life as a handicapped person.

Thirteen

AS soon as Lisa walked into the orthotist's examining room, she saw the brace sitting in the corner. It was a hard plastic tube, longer than in the picture, open in the back, with the two buckles across the opening. It was shaped kind of like her body.

"Yellow today," her mom said as she pulled another undershirt out of a bag she had brought with her. Lisa took it reluctantly. She wished her mom would stop trying to be so cheerful. Lisa slowly pulled off her clothes and put the undershirt on. I guess this is it, she told herself sadly.

When Chris came in, he asked Lisa to stand with her arms straight up over her head. Then he pulled the back edges of the brace apart and helped her squeeze her body through the opening. "Someone will have to help you get this on and off, of course," he mentioned.

The top of the brace was too high, and Lisa couldn't put her arms down. It was too long, so she couldn't move her legs or sit down. She was afraid she would lose her balance and fall!

"I can't move!" she said angrily.

"Hang on a second, Lisa," Chris told her as he quickly marked the brace with a grease pencil. Then he pulled it off and cut it under the arms and at the legs. When he put it back on, Lisa could put her arms down, but the brace was still so tight she could hardly breathe. Chris studied her X rays for a minute, made more marks on the brace, and took it off again.

By the end of the session, Chris had cut the brace so it came just under her right armpit, but much lower on the left side. He had put hard, flat pads inside the brace on the right side at chest level and at the left side at her hip.

"These pads will push against both curves," he explained. "That's how the brace keeps the curves from getting worse."

Mrs. Conklin nodded, but Lisa was so tired and sore from taking the brace on and off that she didn't care anymore.

"Joyce is waiting down the hall at Dr. Burns's office to take X rays of you in the brace," Chris told her. "The X rays will tell us if the pads are in the right place."

When Lisa brought the X rays back to Chris, she hoped they would show the brace was too tight, but they didn't.

"We'd like to see Lisa again in about a month," Chris told Mrs. Conklin, "just to make sure the brace is doing what it's supposed to do. Dr. Burns will want to check her again in a few months, too." He patted Lisa's shoulder. "You were great today, Lisa. I know this isn't a lot of fun."

Lisa stared at the floor. All she wanted to do was go home and hide in her bedroom. The brace made her body feel like a chunk of cement. It was hard to believe she had ever done even one back walkover. Tears kept trying to slip out of her eyes.

As soon as Chris left, Lisa picked up her jeans off a chair. Then she looked down at the brace.

"Mom! My jeans won't fit over this brace!" she said angrily.

"You're right, Lisa," her mom said, "but I brought some clothes that will." Mrs. Conklin reached into her bag again and pulled out pale-blue sweatpants with a drawstring waist and a matching sweatshirt.

"We'll go right to the store from here and get more pants," her mother promised. "The waist just needs to be a little bigger to fit over the brace. All your sweaters and blouses should be okay, but maybe we could buy a few new ones, anyway, to match your new pants.

Lisa slowly pulled on the sweatsuit. She was glad there wasn't a mirror in the room. When she was dressed, her mom pulled her close and hugged her. But with the brace on, Lisa couldn't really feel her mother's body against hers. She felt removed from everything, like she was in a dream.

Lisa followed her mother out to the car. She couldn't remember when she'd felt so tired or so awkward. New clothes can't make up for this, she told herself. I should just get some football jerseys to wear to school. I already look like I'm on the team.

At the store, though, Lisa found some nice pants with elastic in the waistbands. Even baggy jeans a size bigger didn't look too bad, especially with new shirts to go with them. Just as Lisa was beginning to feel a little better, a sales clerk decided to help.

"Well," the clerk said as she peeked around the curtain in the dressing room, "how are we doing?"

Then the clerk saw the white brace showing above the jeans Lisa was trying on. Even her heavy makeup didn't hide the shocked look on her face. Lisa wished she could disappear.

"We don't need any help," Mrs. Conklin told the clerk.

The clerk couldn't seem to take her eyes off the brace. "Well, I don't think our clothes would fit handicapped people anyway. Maybe maternity clothes would hide that . . . that . . ."

Lisa turned away from her stare and leaned her head against the wall. The hot tears she had held back all afternoon started sliding down her cheeks. Mrs. Conklin stepped between Lisa and the clerk.

"You should be more concerned with your own 'handicap' as you put it," she told the clerk.

The woman gasped and drew herself up as tall as possible. "I don't have a handicap of any kind!" she insisted.

"Yes, you do," Mrs. Conklin told her. Her mother spoke very quietly, but Lisa could hear the anger in her voice. "Your handicap is your rudeness and nothing can hide that!"

The clerk opened her mouth to say something, but no words came out.

"If I see your face one more time before we leave this store," Mrs. Conklin added, "I will personally speak to your supervisor about your inexcusable remarks."

Without another word, the clerk pulled her head out of the changing room and snapped the curtain closed. Lisa could hear her footsteps clicking quickly down the hall.

Lisa's mom pulled her close again. "Lisa," she said softly, "it doesn't matter what that stupid woman thinks. We're not going to let her ruin our shopping trip. Now, should we buy the clothes we've picked out? Or should we leave them here and go to another store where the clerks are human beings?"

Lisa looked at the piles of clothes she had chosen. Her tears made the bright colors seem as if they were running together. "Let's buy these, Mom," she finally said. She just wanted to go home.

Riding in the car, a huge bag of clothes in the back seat behind her, Lisa wondered if the kids at school would treat her like the sales clerk had. She didn't think she could stand it.

Fourteen

"LET me stay home today. I need more time to get used to this brace," Lisa begged her parents the next morning.

"Lisa," her father said gently, "you have to go to school today. If you don't want to walk, I'll drop you off. The only thing the kids are going to notice is how great you look in your new clothes."

Lisa had already spent a long time staring at herself in the full-length mirror in her bedroom. She had to admit she couldn't actually see the brace under her new sweater. Her new pants had elastic in the waistband, so they looked almost normal, too. Still, someone might bump against me and feel this hard brace under my sweater, she worried.

Mrs. Conklin kissed her daughter's cheek. "You can't miss school today, honey. This is the day you're going to find out that no one knows or cares that you're wearing a brace."

Lisa frowned at her mother. Sure, Mom, she wanted to say, just like the clerk at the store!

She jammed her arms into her coat and grabbed her school bag. I do know what day this is, she told herself: It's the day I'll find out if I have any friends at all.

After her father dropped her at school, Lisa thought about wearing her coat all day long to help hide the brace. But she was too hot, so she slipped it off and hung it in her locker. Then she waited until almost the last bell to go to her first class. I'll just wait for the crowd in the halls to clear a little, she decided. The fewer people around, the better.

Just as the tardy bell rang, Lisa stiffly sat down in her seat in English class.

"Hi, Lisa!" someone behind her whispered.

Oh, great, Lisa thought. I forgot Patti sits behind me in this class. Patti always has the latest outfit. I'll bet Patti would die before she would wear a brace.

Lisa sat as straight as possible so Patti wouldn't see any ridge across her back from the brace. After a few minutes her muscles hurt from pushing her shoulders back, but she couldn't quit. Just then she heard Patti giggle. She can see it anyway, Lisa thought.

"Lisa! Lisa Conklin!" It was the teacher!

How long had the teacher been calling her? Lisa felt a wave of hotness spread up her neck and over her face.

The teacher walked over and stood by Lisa's desk. "Lisa, now that I finally have your attention, please do the first exercise on page 231," she said.

Lisa nodded and quickly thumbed through her English book. She knew her face was red, and her stomach felt awful. This is a great start to a wonderful day, she told herself. I wonder what the teacher would do if I threw up on her shoes?

Finally, it was lunchtime. Lisa was one of the last ones in the cafeteria so Megan was already waiting at their usual table. Thank goodness Steve isn't there, Lisa told herself. She tried to thread her way between the tables without touching anything.

"Hey! I like your new sweater! And your pants!" Megan said as Lisa reached their table. "Do you think I could borrow them some time?"

Lisa awkwardly sat down. She glared at Megan. She's trying to pretend she doesn't notice the brace, Lisa decided. Nice try!

"What's wrong?" Megan asked in surprise. "If you don't want me to wear your clothes, I won't. I do have clothes of my own, you know."

Ignoring Megan, Lisa dumped her lunch out of the bag. Her orange rolled off the table and onto the floor. She started to bend down to get it, but the brace cut into the top of her legs. She couldn't reach the orange without kneeling on the floor!

Lisa closed her eyes to keep the tears in. I give up, she told herself. This is too hard. I'm going to the nurse's office and say I'm sick. I am sick, really and truly. My whole body hurts, including my heart.

"Lisa, please talk to me," Megan begged.

Lisa opened her eyes. "If you were my friend, Megan, you would admit you see it!" she whispered hoarsely.

Megan stared at her best friend's face. "Lisa, that pimple's been gone for a week!"

"Pimple? What pimple?" Lisa asked.

"Pimple? Who's got pimples?" It was Steve! And Jeff was right behind him, looking down at her with those blue eyes! Lisa stared into her lap. If I can only disappear once in my life, she prayed, let it be now.

"Hi, Steve!" Megan said. Lisa thought she sounded relieved to have someone normal to talk to. "Hi, Jeff!"

"What's for lunch today, Meg?" Steve asked as he slid into the seat beside her. He picked up her lunch bag and peeked in. Megan laughed and handed him her apple.

Lisa didn't look up, but she felt Jeff move closer to her.

"Hi, Lisa," Jeff said. "Are you ready for the math test today?"

Lisa glared at him. "I suppose you don't notice either."

Jeff backed away a step. Megan and Steve stopped talking and looked at Lisa.

"I really like your sweater," Jeff said. "Is that what I'm supposed to notice?" He turned to Steve for help. Steve just shook his head in confusion.

Lisa looked at the circle of puzzled faces. "Pretending everything is all right isn't helping me!" she said through her teeth.

"Uhhh . . . I . . . I don't think Lisa feels too good today, guys," Megan told the boys. She smiled at them nervously, still watching Lisa out of the corner of her eye.

"You're right, Megan!" Lisa hissed. "I think I'm going to be sick!" Lisa got up and ran for the girls' restroom. A minute later she stood looking into one of the toilets, trying to decide whether she really was going to throw up.

The restroom door opened. "Lisa!" Megan called. "Where are you? Are you really sick? Should I get the nurse?"

"I don't need the nurse!" Lisa yelled back.

Luckily no one else was in the restroom. "I need a real friend! Somebody who will admit I look like a freak and like me anyway!'

"Lisa!" Megan said. "I don't know what you're talking about! I'm going to get the nurse!" Lisa heard the restroom door open.

She really doesn't know I'm wearing the brace! Lisa finally realized. She really can't see it! She must think I've lost my mind!

Lisa opened the stall door. "Wait, Megan!" she yelled. Megan was holding the restroom door open. She looked so confused that Lisa started to giggle.

"Lisa!" Megan said in desperation. "Why are you laughing now?"

Lisa stopped laughing long enough to make a fist and knock hard on the brace under her sweater. The rapping sound was muffled by her sweater, but it surprised Megan anyway.

"What's that sound?" Megan asked. She let the restroom door close.

"It's my brace!" Lisa said between giggles. She wasn't sure now whether she was laughing or crying.

"Oh, you got your brace!" Megan gasped. She walked over to Lisa. "That's what's bothering you! I forgot, Lisa! I'm sorry! I was so busy thinking about Steve." She bit her lip and looked Lisa up and down. "I can't tell! I thought I would be able to see it. Why didn't you just tell me?"

"I thought you could see it—see that I'm different!" Lisa said. Suddenly she was fighting not to cry.

Megan smiled and hugged her friend. She laughed when she felt the hard plastic under the new sweater. "All I saw was your new sweater!" Megan told her. "It looks like it's just my size!"

Fifteen

JUST as Lisa and Megan walked back in the cafeteria, the bell rang. They grabbed their books off their table and hurried out.

"Jeff and Steve must have already gone to math class," Megan said breathlessly as they rushed through the halls. "I wish I had studied more for this test!"

I wish I hadn't acted so weird in front of Jeff, Lisa thought. I'll bet he's afraid to talk to me now.

As Lisa stiffly lowered herself into her seat in math class, she could see Jeff sitting three rows in front of her. He glanced back at her once, with a questioning look in his blue eyes. Lisa smiled quickly, but he had already turned around. Just then the teacher told them to put their books under their seats and get ready for the test.

No wonder Jeff's confused, Lisa told herself

He really doesn't know about the brace. He must think I'm crazy! I guess I am acting kind of strangely.

Lisa tried to concentrate on the test, but halfway through it she realized that she had gym class next. Oh, no, she groaned. She'd forgotten all about it. She'd never be able to get in and out of her brace by the time the class started. And if she left it on in the locker room, everyone would see it. She thought about it for a second and then decided just to leave it on. At least, they were playing volleyball in gym. She could probably play okay with the brace on.

Finally, Lisa finished writing numbers in all the answer spaces on her math test. Who knows? she thought. Maybe some of these answers are right.

The bell rang. Lisa saw Jeff hurry out to his next class. She reluctantly headed for the gym, walking close to the walls in the hallways so no one would bump her.

A few minutes later, as she pulled her old sweatpants and T-shirt out of her gym locker, she remembered all the times she had worn those same clothes for gym. She had always been the star of the class. Now she dreaded putting them on.

In the noisy locker room the girls in her

class were spread out along the double row of lockers, talking and laughing and tossing clothes everywhere as they hurried to change. Lisa pulled her new pants below her hips and sat down on the bench that ran in front of the lockers. She was careful to keep her sweater over the brace. Then she slipped the pants off her feet and pulled her gym sweats on.

Lisa looked down at the T-shirt in her hand.

She couldn't figure out how to get it on without taking her sweater off She even considered putting it on feet-first, but then she decided that pulling the T-shirt up over her hips wouldn't work out too well, brace or no brace. Lisa finally went into the restroom to finish changing. No one seemed to notice.

As she walked out of the restroom, someone yelled, "Hey, Lisa!" She jerked her head toward the voice. It was Ann from gymnastics. Had she seen the brace?

"We're working on the balance beam in gym today!" Ann called. She hadn't seen the brace! "Maybe Miss Williams will need our help again!"

The volleyball unit we were studying must be over. Now what am I going to do? she thought.

Lisa remembered how Miss Williams had

asked her to demonstrate a cartwheel on the beam the last time. What if she does that again? she worried. What will I say?

The teacher was already in the gym when Lisa followed the last of her class in. Lisa noticed Miss Williams was wearing her yellow sweatsuit today, with a matching yellow ribbon tied around her ponytail. Lisa had always thought gray hair looked strange in a ponytail. Today she decided Miss Williams could wear her hair in a Mohawk if she wanted to, as long as she didn't ask Lisa to demonstrate anything.

The teacher motioned for the girls to come where she was standing, by the balance beam. The beam was low, only about four inches off the floor. As the girls gathered around the beam, Lisa tried to hide behind some of the taller kids in her class.

"Today we're going to practice forward somersaults on the low beam," Miss Williams told them. "They're a little difficult, but I want you all to try them. Now, I'm a little old for this," she paused and some of the girls giggled, "but we've got some real gymnastic pros in this class, so I'm going to ask them to help me up here."

Lisa held her breath. The teacher searched through the crowd of girls. "Ann, would you come up here, please?" she asked.

That was close! Lisa thought. She watched Ann smile and walk up to stand beside Miss Williams.

"Lisa? Lisa Conklin? Are you here today?" Miss Williams called.

Lisa's heart sank. Patti was standing near her. She giggled and poked Lisa in the ribs with her elbow. Patti's mouth dropped open when her elbow hit the hard brace under Lisa's T-shirt. Lisa didn't even notice. She was paralyzed.

"Lisa? Will you help me today?" Miss Williams had spotted her. Everyone else was looking at her, too.

Lisa swallowed hard and looked at the floor. "I can't, Miss Williams," she mumbled. The words seemed to catch in her throat.

The other girls had moved aside to make a path between Lisa and the teacher. "Why not, Lisa?" Miss Williams asked in a puzzled voice. "I've seen you do some moves on the balance beam that no one else here can do. You must be able to do forward somersaults in your sleep!"

Lisa slowly raised her eyes to face her teacher. She could feel the stares of the other girls. Someone was whispering behind her.

Then, for some reason, Lisa thought of the twisted, hunched-over woman she had seen in

Dr. Killinger's office. Then she remembered the picture of her mother in the thick cast, a cast that Lisa would probably never have to wear because of the brace.

Lisa swallowed hard. I'm going to have to face this sooner or later, she decided. I can't spend the next four years hiding my brace.

She took a deep breath. "I have scoliosis," she told Miss Williams and everyone else there. "I have to wear a brace to help my back grow straight, so I can't do somersaults anymore." Lisa paused for a second and blinked back the tears that threatened to spill out of her eyes. She held her chin higher. "But I can help the other girls learn how."

Lisa walked up to stand beside Miss Williams and Ann. No one spoke. Lisa had never heard the gym so quiet.

Finally Miss Williams broke the silence. "Thanks, Lisa. I really need your help." She put her arm around Lisa's shoulders and hugged her. Lisa heard her whisper, "I'm proud of you."

After gym class, when the girls ran back into the locker room to change, a small crowd gathered around Lisa. "How long have you been wearing the brace?" Patti asked. "I couldn't even tell!"

Ann hugged Lisa. "I'll really miss you at

gymnastics, Lisa!" Her eyes looked misty. "You were the best of us all!"

Lisa smiled a genuine smile for the first time in a long time. I really do miss being at the gym, she thought. "You won't miss me much longer," she said. "I'm going to coach the beginner's class for Mrs. Pogue!" Lisa surprised herself when she said it. Then she thought, why not? I belong in that gym, one way or another.

"Hey," someone said, "we'd better change! The bell's going to ring!"

All the girls rushed to their lockers except one, a quiet girl named Jill. "I have scoliosis, too," Jill told Lisa softly. "The doctor takes X rays every six months." She held up both hands with her fingers crossed and smiled. "So far, so good."

Lisa smiled back. "That's great! But if your curve starts getting worse, don't worry. Wearing a brace isn't much fun, but it's not the end of the world!" And Lisa realized as she said it that she really almost meant it.

During her last class of the day Lisa had no idea what her language teacher was talking about. The brace was still uncomfortable, but she felt a little better knowing that everyone knew. And the more she thought about coaching the beginner's class, the more excited she became. Maybe she could start tonight! Then she remembered it was Friday night. The swim party . . .

After language class, Lisa hurried to the lockers. She saw Jeff standing by himself, getting his coat out.

"Jeff!" she called as she hurried toward him.

He turned and looked almost shocked to see her. "Uh, hi, Lisa. Uh, I'm sorry about lunch today. I always say the wrong things to girls." He kicked a piece of paper on the floor. "

"It was all my fault, Jeff. You didn't say anything wrong."

"Well," he smiled shyly, "I usually do."

"Jeff, I . . . ," Lisa began, but Jeff interrupted her. "Lisa, maybe I shouldn't say this either, but didn't you tell me you were going to get your brace this week?"

"I already have my brace," she told him. "I'm wearing it!" She knocked on her ribs again. Jeff's mouth dropped open in surprise. Lisa smiled. "I thought you knew at lunchtime. I thought you were just pretending not to see it. That's why I acted so crazy. I'm sorry.

Jeff shook his head. "I never guessed you were wearing a brace." Then he smiled at her. "You always look great to me!"

Lisa stared at him for a long moment. He was wearing a shirt that looked so soft she wanted to touch it. It was the same blue as his eyes. He was standing so close she could smell his cologne or soap or whatever made him smell so good.

Lisa took as deep a breath as she could in the tight brace. "Are you going to the swim party tonight?" she asked.

"Not unless you are," he answered. Lisa's heart leaped in her chest. She was so excited she could hardly breathe.

"I'll go," she said as calmly as she could. "Maybe I'll even join the girls' swim team. I hear swimming is good exercise."

Jeff smiled again and shyly took her hand in his. "Could I walk you home?" he asked.

Lisa nodded. It was going to be all right, she thought to herself. Wearing this brace isn't going to be easy, but I'll get through it, one day at a time.

She felt Jeff's hand in hers and looked into his eyes. She hoped the walk home would last the rest of her life!

Scoliosis—Some Facts

- Scoliosis is a side-to-side curving of the spine.
- About 1 in 10 people have a mild form of scoliosis.
- Scoliosis may progress rapidly during the adolescent growth years, between the ages of 10 and 15.
- Scoliosis can be most effectively treated if detected early. Left untreated, scoliosis can cause physical deformity, pain, arthritic symptoms, heart and lung complications, and can limit physical activity.
- Frequent signs of scoliosis are:
  —A prominent shoulder blade;
  —Uneven hip and shoulder levels;
  —Unequal distance between arms and body;
  —Clothes that do not hang right.
- Treatment for mild scoliosis usually involves observing the curve to make sure that it does not worsen. For curves that are progressing, treatment may involve a body brace. In severe cases, surgery may be necessary.

For more information write to:

National Scoliosis Foundation
72 Mount Auburn Street
Watertown, MA 02172

About the Author

"When people learn I have scoliosis, they may wonder how much of this book is true," Linda Barr says. "Actually, all of it is, but some of it happened to other people."

Linda had her first spinal surgery when she was 12, to fuse her top curve. Her lower curve continued to progress, however, and she had her second surgery when she was 39, to fuse the rest of her spine. By then the lower curve measured 73 degrees.

When Linda was almost finished writing this book, her family doctor detected a slight curve in her own daughter's spine. Linda took eleven-year-old Colleen to a scoliosis specialist who monitored Colleen for nearly four years, taking X rays two or three times a year. Fortunately, Colleen's curve did not progress past about 12 degrees, which is common for most people with scoliosis, so she didn't need any treatment.

"Doctors know so much more about scoliosis now," she says. "With early diagnosis and treatment, very few kids need surgery and casts and long stays in hospital beds. I hope young people who need treatment for their scoliosis will get it. They'll be glad they did for the rest of their lives, believe me!"

The author, a freelance writer, lives in Columbus, Ohio, with her husband Tom, son Dan, daughter Colleen, and a parrot named Kermit.